# SACHIN'S CREED

# SACHIN'S CREED
## THE HUNDRED

ANDREW WILLIAM HARTSHORN

Matador
9 Priory Business Park,
Wistow Road, Kibworth Beauchamp,
Leicestershire. LE8 0RX
Tel: 0116 279 2299
Email: books@troubador.co.uk
Web: www.troubador.co.uk/matador
Twitter: @matadorbooks

ISBN 978 1800 46491 9

British Library Cataloguing in Publication Data.
A catalogue record for this book is available from the British Library.

Printed and bound in Great Britain by 4edge Limited
Typeset in 12pt Adobe Garamond Pro by Troubador Publishing Ltd,
Leicester, UK

Matador is an imprint of Troubador Publishing Ltd

For my Dad.

# CHAPTER 1

As the entire Dulkar family watched the England cricket team battle for a draw with India at Edgbaston on their giant sixty-five inch, widescreen television, Sachin noticed his school mate George outside the window.

Sachin went to open the door of number 10, Wibble Street. He caught George waiting for his pal Billy from number 11. George was teasing a black and white pentagon clad football to and fro against the grimy kerb.

Mr. Dulkar was heard shouting in the background, 'HOWZAT!' George was unfamiliar with the word. Sachin knew 'HOWZAT!' as the first word that he ever heard and was, apparently, the first word that he ever uttered.

George gestured to Sachin, by flapping his hands, for him to come out and play footie but Sachin explained, "I cannot come out now we're going shopping and I am watching the cricket."

George tried to persuade him, "You can go shopping any time Sachin!"

"No chance! We're all watching the cricket anyway.

My brothers and mother all have to shop for school stuff later," insisted Sachin.

Sachin had seven brothers, some of them were away at university but he and three other brothers still lived at number ten.

"School will be starting soon and mother wants us all ready. With brothers like mine we ALL have to work hard," Sachin continued.

"Okay mate. Perhaps we can do something soon," George said, keen to add to his very short tally of pals.

Sachin smiled and explained he had to go as his father was shouting because there had been another wicket in the cricket. He quickly retreated back behind the door to be greeted by his brothers reluctantly applauding India's latest wicket. Mr. Dulkar was hoping for an Indian fightback. All his sons were born in England and their instinct was to be loyal to the cause of the English team.

They all played cricket. They watched cricket. They lived for cricket. It was the last few days of the summer and the brothers had spent most of their spare time with a bat and a ball close to them. Sachin was the youngest of the children. At eleven years of age he dreamed of playing cricket for England, for India, for anyone!

He was as good as any of his elder brothers, who all played for a team somewhere, at some level. Sachin had played mainly Kwik-cricket for his school and other forms of the sport at Skaggyness Cricket Club. He had also just returned from a summer coaching school at Lord's, in London (or just around the corner from

Sherlock Holmes's house as he tells people), the home of English cricket.

He had been coached using a lethal weapon; which a cricket ball could be. He had borrowed all the equipment from his brothers. He had sweated for a month in slightly long white trousers, a too big white polo-shirt and an over baggy white jumper. The helmet fell-off on a regular basis, despite him pulling the chin strap super tight. The ball had pinged off his head a couple of times but he hadn't cared! He had been learning how to play the game he was in love with.

When he returned from London to Skaggyness for the last week of the holidays, he decided to keep his 'lucky' cricket pads on. They were 'lucky' pads simply because the batting coach had an old spare pair that his son had outgrown them. So lucky for Sachin, he gave them to him, who had none of his own.

Mr.Dulkar, Sachin's father, had brought-up all his sons to understand the game of cricket and the importance of playing to the rules. He had also instilled in them that cricket would teach them many life skills. His father insisted that he would learn more from failure than from success.

He told Sachin that it was more important than anything else, to his mother and himself that people spoke of him in a positive way.

Sachin didn't always understand his father's lecture's but he knew not to listen to him would be a mistake. One thing he was sure of was that he loved his father and thanked him daily for helping him find a passion for cricket.

# CHAPTER 2

The phone rang and Mr. Dulkar was having a very animated conversation with someone as he continued to have one eye on the television; which wasn't difficult as the television was so big it filled a whole wall of the lounge on its own.

Mr. Dulkar was one of the board members of Skaggyness Cricket Club. Skaggyness C.C. were a struggling, poor, cricket club with teams at several levels including an under-16 team. Sachin was desperate to play in the under sixteen side as that was the youngest level of side the club ran.

Skaggyness played their matches in the shadows of the Olympic Superstore Stadium (the home of Skaggyness Albion Football Club). They were allowed to use the football club's changing facilities and had what looked like a giant shipwreck as a pavilion. It was a place where Mr. Dulkar spent a good deal of his spare time doing anything he could to help the club. He was very well thought of by everyone who met him. A polite, kind hearted gentleman of the town.

Beston Cricket Club were the local rivals from the next town. They had the very best of everything. They didn't have to borrow changing rooms or check that the 'shipwreck' of a pavilion would fall down if you were to open the door just a little-too-quickly. Mr. Dulkar hated playing Beston. Not only did Skaggyness regularly lose to Beston, at all levels, Mr. Dulkar's beastly, boastful cousin, Sunil Ganguly, was Chairman of the Beston club.

Every family gathering brought Mr. Dulkar and his cousin Ganguly together in the same room. Mr. Dulkar had for many years now had to suffer the Ganguly smugness as at every wedding, birthday party and even funeral. Cousin Sunil had never let an opportunity pass to remind Mr. Dulkar of Beston's latest 'thrashing' of Skaggyness.

Mr.Dulkar was always embarrassed to listen to Ganguly's boasting which never stopped at a rerun of every key shot or wicket of the latest match. His jibes extended to 'our grass on our pitch is greener than yours', 'our pavilion is a palace not a patched up disaster like your excuse for a pavilion' and 'our players don't like to come and play in Skaggyness, they feel it's like playing in a rubbish dump!'

In the past Mr.Dulkar and Ganguly had been rivals on the pitch a long time before they were rivals off it. Once upon a time, they had been like brothers. That all changed when Ganguly was appointed captain of his boys club in Mumbai; back in India. The two cousins had been friendly rivals until, at the age of fifteen, they met in a boys club clash in for the first time since Ganguly had been made captain.

Ganguly was constantly goading Mr. Dulkar reminding him of all his shortcomings. His put downs and insults, in front of everybody, were nasty and personal. Ganguly had turned into a vile bully.

In that one match, as a fifteen-year old, their friendship ended as Ganguly was determined to hurt Mr. Dulkar with the world watching. When Mr. Dulkar came out to bat in that game, his cousin was determined to make him look like a fool.

Mr. Dulkar's side were struggling in the match before he came out to bat. When he came out Ganguly decided it was time for him bowl. Mr. Dulkar took guard ready for his cousin to run in. Ganguly came charging in, like a rampant stag. At first, Mr.Dulkar was convinced he had been bowled a beamer.

Mr. Dulkar didn't even see the ball leave his hand. He had expected to be hit on the head at any moment because he hadn't seen the ball at all. Ganguly thought it was a huge joke because he had run in without a ball in his hand. Ganguly stood there, arms folded, laughing like a hyena as his team mates pointed at Mr.Dulkar 'the fool'.

Mr.Dulkar did not think that this act of tomfoolery was funny at all!

Mr.Dulkar didn't believe in retaliating with his mouth. He always believed actions speak louder than words and told Sachin he should think the same way. He started to hit his cousins' team's bowling all over the ground. After the ball had crossed the boundary rope for the umpteenth time, Ganguly lost his cool.

He strode down the pitch, stood square in front of Mr.Dulkar and let out the most enormous rasping FART!

Glaring at his cousin, Ganguly snarled, "Try hitting that for six!"

The friendship between the two was very much over and their rivalry had very much begun.

The conflict was about to spark again. The annual Skegness versus Beston under-sixteen match was due to take place in Skaggyness in just a few days. Mr. Dulkar had had a very intense conversation on the phone. He was wearing a very concerned look on his face. He called out…

"Sachin! Sachin! Come here quickly!"

Sachin waved at him, as he was standing by the room's exit with a glass of milk making its home in his hands.

"Sachin my boy! We have a problem! We only have seven players for the Beston match next week. Coach Joe says he wants you to play. Are you ready?"

"Ready? I have been ready since I was born father!" gasped Sachin.

Mr. Dulkar wasn't so worried about Sachin's ability, he knew he was a decent cricketer for his age, but he was worried that Ganguly would target him. Mr.Dulkar's first instinct was to protect his son. In many previous matches, that any of his other sons had played against a team connected to Ganguly, his sons had been given an 'extra-warm', or even toxic, welcome from the other team. The greeting was often so warm you could say they had had a roasting!

Sachin was only eleven and that meant he was already up against older, bigger and stronger players. Sachin knew that this fact would bother his father.

Sachin looked at his dad for a few moments before declaring, "Its okay father, I am a TIGER!"

His father smiled a nervous smile and responded, "Yes…yes you are my son."

"ROARRRRRR!" Sachin cried.

Mr. Dulkar, although reluctant, agreed that it was his time to step-up to face the older boys.

"That leaves us still three players short. Do you know anyone Sachin?" Mr. Dulkar enquired. He put the question again to Sachin's brothers, blank looks and silence aplenty.

"What about the two boys you waved at in our street Sachin? We only have two days before the match!" The Skaggyness versus Beston cricket match, at all levels, always took place on a bank holiday Monday.

Sachin was ruthless when it came to his precious cricket. It was the reason he got up in the morning. He took it super seriously. Sachin suggested that the two boys wouldn't be interested and probably couldn't play anyway. Mr. Dulkar urged Sachin to investigate and stressed, "We're desperate!"

Mr. Dulkar probed Sachin for the boys' names and Sachin explained that George was the red headed boy from number one and the other boy was from number eleven, the street's new family. Mr. Dulkar did not rest on the information. He quickly put on his white cloth cap and disappeared out of the house.

# CHAPTER 3

M r. Dulkar returned to the place where the goggle box continued to strain to the commentator's overture. Sachin was waiting, clutching one of his cricket bats that he had been pretending to swat away the imaginary bowling of the Beston attack only moments earlier.

"Those boys will play. Their parents say okay. The boy Billy is very keen. His parents are jolly nice people. That George boy, awfully strange kid. His father said it will do him good to get a battering! Strange fellow, odd family!" screeched Mr. Dulkar.

"Do they know how to play?" Sachin enquired.

"Ah. That is a point. Billy is a bit of a sporty one and can play a little. The red kid, according to his father, couldn't catch a cold, can't hit a wall and will run from the ball as if it's a bomb," Mr. Dulkar explained.

"You're meeting them tomorrow at the pavilion, at ten o'clock to give them some coaching and practise. Don't be late, we need to work them hard to be ready for Monday!" Mr. Dulkar reminded him.

Sachin nodded obediently. 'Roll on tomorrow', he thought to himself. He also pondered, that even with Billy and George the team was still one short.

# Chapter 4

Sachin lay motionless in his bed. He had been wide awake since early light. He was staring at the poster of the England cricket team. He was imagining that he was opening the batting in the World Cup Final against India or Australia or Sri Lanka or New Zealand. He couldn't be sure who they would be playing so he dreamed each day that the final would be against different opposition.

Sachin got up to shower and he was thinking about how he had a coaching responsibility to George and Billy. He was hoping he could be able to teach them something, at least how to hold a bat properly.

He arrived at the pavilion at eight o'clock in the morning. Always keen, Sachin seized the opportunity to check kit and equipment for his probable team mates. He sorted out different size bats, jumpers, trousers, helmets and pads.

He then grabbed hold of the nearest passer-by and persuaded them to bowl a few at him in the nets. It was Ben who was the lucky player today. Ben was delighted to help Sachin out. Now Ben was a player Sachin had a great admiration for. He was a first teamer for Skaggyness and an all-rounder, meaning he was a key batsmen and bowler. In Ben, Skaggyness had a top, top fielder as well. Apart from the wicket keeper, Ben had more catches to his name each season than any player.

Sachin was focused on Ben bowling gently at him while he got his eye in. Sachin was explaining the situation to Ben in regards to the predicament of the under-16 side. Ben sympathised but had no answer for him. "I can stick around and help coach your new boys for an hour this morning, if you think it would help," offered Ben. Sachin explained that it would be a help.

Both Ben and Sachin watched in wonder as the two budding cricketers approached them for their ten o'clock appointment. They weren't late so that was a good start!

When the introductions were over the boys began to learn about the equipment. They were taught how to throw and catch the ball properly.

After half-an-hour they paused for a breather. Sachin asked both Billy and George what they knew about the rules of cricket. The two boys looked at each other blankly. Sachin asked them if they could bat or bowl at all. The two boys continued their well exercised blank looks. Sachin asked them, "Do you know anything about cricket at all?" again vacant faces.

Billy chirped, "When the batsman hits the ball you have to stop it from going over the boundary and then throw it back to the stumps. Or better still catch the ball so that the batsman is OUT!"

"Correct!" yelped Sachin as he breathed a sigh of relief that at least one of the two new recruits had at least some idea about how the game of cricket is played.

With his head bowed and staring forlornly at the floor, George noted, "I think we have got a lot to learn but we want to do our best for you Sachin."

"You will boys, I'm sure you'll do your bit," added Ben.

"We still need another player. Beston are an excellent side and we definitely need one more," Sachin informed the two boys enquiring if they knew anyone.

The boys continued their blank looks.

Sachin sighed. He badly wanted to win against Beston…for his father's sake if not for the simple joy of winning.

Ben left the boys to it as he had to shoot. Sachin thanked him and turned to the boys to continue their cricket education.

Sachin suggested a cola or lemonade from the vending machine. They drank and they talked with Billy buying drinks for all.

Sachin began his lecture, "Cricket is played by two teams of eleven players or at least our match and adult versions of the game are. Thirteen players will be involved in the play at any one time: two batters from one team, and a bowler, wicketkeeper and nine fielders from the opposing team."

"Which version of cricket will we be playing?" enquired Billy.

"Will it last five-days?" asked George.

"No it won't last five days, it is not Test cricket! I never stopped to ask my father which format we're going to play but it will be a short form in the afternoon, in the beating Sun," insisted Sachin.

"It's too hot now! It's only morning!" noted George.

Sachin continued his lecture, "I am sure though that whatever format we play it will be made-up of two innings, which means that each team will bat and bowl against the other. An innings lasts for a set amount of overs, or until 10 batters are out. The aim of the game is to score more runs than the opposition."

"What are runs?" inquired George.

"They're the same as points that are scored by the batting team. They're called runs because most of them are earned by running between the two sets of sticks on the field," Billy confidently replied to George.

Sachin added, "You're right but you can also earn runs by boundaries and extras, and the sticks, as you call them are called wickets."

"Okay, so if we, if we're batting hit the ball and run to the opposite end of the pitch, this counts as a run, right?" George asserted.

"Correct" said Sachin.

Billy added, "If the batter then runs back to the starting end, the score is two, and so on, right?"

"You guys are learning quickly. A batter may run as many times as he or she likes, but must avoid being run out by the fielding team. Both batters need to run for runs to be scored, so you will cross over in the middle of the pitch. Batters can be run out if they fail to make their ground, get to the other end of the pitch that is," explained Sachin.

"Will we get to throw the ball at any batters when we are fielding?" asked Billy.

"You mean bowl, I think. Can you bowl?" inquired Sachin.

"I have had a go before," said Billy.

"Let's go and give you both an over and see how you go," suggested Sachin.

The three moved over to the nets where a pitch with wickets was set up for practise sessions. The purpose of the net was simply to ensure the ball did not travel too far and could easily be retrieved.

Sachin kitted George out with pads, helmet and bat as he prepared him to face some bowling. He was careful to teach him how to hold his bat correctly and taught him a simple defensive stroke.

Billy watched carefully waiting for his turn for action. Sachin then explained how to bowl within the laws of cricket. Sachin explained that cricket is broken down into units called overs. An over consists of six legal deliveries bowled consecutively by a single bowler from the same end of the pitch.

So Sachin, bowled six nice easy deliveries to George. George thrilling at simply getting his bat to tap the ball away, he was so proud. Billy made him work harder with more power behind his bowling, George finding them much harder to hit.

The two trainee cricketers switched roles. Sachin noted their efforts. "Not bad for learners boys, not bad."

Sachin explained more about scoring runs. He walked them round the whole pitch and explained where fielders should go. He pointed out to the sun kissed turf and used the sprinklers that were hard at work as reference points to his guide. Sachin pointed out the boundary, "This is the perimeter of the outfield, here look, it's where the rope is. If the ball goes over the boundary without bouncing the batter automatically scores six runs. If the ball makes contact with the ground after being struck and then goes over the boundary, four runs are scored."

He explained extras, no balls and wides; byes and leg byes.

"How do we know when to stop batting?" asked George.

Sachin explained how you can get 'out'. "You'll stop batting when you're out. That means that you might have been bowled; the ball hits your stumps on your wicket. Or you're caught by a fielder before the ball hits the ground after the ball has been struck by your bat or maybe your glove."

He continued, "Of course there is also leg before wicket. LBW. Sachin took a few minutes to explain LBW. The empty looks made an unwelcome return to George and Billy's faces as they were completely lost with this particular way of getting out. Sachin assured them that they would practise more before the match.

"You can also be stumped, run out, hit wicket and dismissed for handling the ball and obstructing the field."

"Don't fret boys, the umpire will let you know if you're out. You just have to try and hit the ball and score runs."

"What's the Empire?" asked George.

"UMPIRE!" exclaimed Billy, "Cricket referee!"

George made him a heartfelt promise, "We'll try Sachin mate, we'll try."

Sachin took the boys into the pavilion. Mrs. Dulkar was there. She gestured to the boys to help themselves to homemade samosas and curried egg sandwiches.

Mrs. Dulkar asked if the boys were enjoying learning how to play cricket. The two colourful boys commented on how clever Sachin was where cricket was concerned. "He is a fanatic! Like all of my boys!" she declared.

The two boys said they were learning and hoped they could help the team out.

"We're still a player short!" chirped Mr. Dulkar who was lurking in the background.

"How are these two youngsters doing Sachin? Can they cut the cricket mustard?"

"They're trying their best and they're learning quickly!" Sachin stuck-up for his two supportive pals.

"Your dad is very serious about this match isn't he," commented Billy whispering to Sachin. Sachin explained to Billy all about the rivalry between his dad and his Uncle. "I thought it was just a boy's cricket match," added Billy.

"Not just boys, some girls play as well. Cricket is like war for my dad and my Uncle," Sachin stated.

"Now I get the picture," Billy attested.

The two boys vowed to meet Sachin again tomorrow for more practise and coaching, promising to take up cricket arms in the struggle for this family pride.

Billy had been thinking about the fact that the team were still one player short. He had been thinking about all the boys he knew that could play cricket, that lived in Skaggyness and that was a long list of nil. Now he knew that girls were allowed to play, that changed his thinking.

# CHAPTER 5

As the two walked home, Billy asked George about the seven sisters that lived at number seven Wibble Street. George, as always on this subject, advised him that these girls were dangerous and they should avoid all contact. Billy always felt that this was an extreme view but on his meetings with them he had noted that they were full of spirit.

"How about your sister?" enquired George.

"My little pesky sister? No chance! She is too young! She is a fast runner but simply too small and young for this task. But what about your sisters? They are older than mine."

George explained that his dad wouldn't let either of them play in such a game. He told Billy how his dad had only allowed him to play when he his dad had learned that his son might get hurt by a 'real' cricket ball. 'Nice dad!' thought Billy.

"I am going to ask the girls at number seven. I bet they're up for it!" insisted Billy.

"We will go back in the morning and meet Sachin. I might, by then, have our last player," suggested Billy.

# Chapter 6

Billy had had no hesitation in knocking on the door to number seven Wibble Street that evening. He wasn't the type of boy to be easily scared by anything. Despite all the warnings from George about the seven sisters, he was keen to find out more. After knocking, waiting, knocking, waiting and knocking some more eventually he had been greeted from the other side of the door by a voice, "What d'ya want?"

Billy bent down to meet eye-to-eye through the letterbox with what he thought might be the eyes of something from a monster movie. He could hear cackling all around from the back of the eyes. A booming voice from the rear of the troop exclaimed, "We are the wicked witches of Skaggyness, do you want to become our evil little pet?"

Completely undeterred, Billy explained that he needed help. The girls were listening, a little disappointed at his apparent bravery. The girls were used to people being scared of them and enjoyed terrorising boys whenever they could.

"We will help you our evil little pet! But what will you do for us?" the booming voice went on.

Billy suggested that he would do anything they wanted. The door eased itself open. The girls had decided that if the boy wasn't going to run, then they might as well open-up to have some fun.

He was greeted by seven scowling faces. He looked all around them waiting for fear to come; it did not. He saw seven girls of all ages, shapes and sizes. He was looking around trying to work out which one was most likely to become his new team mate. They all stared at him. They were looking him up and down. Bashing Bonnie was the owner of the booming voice. She spoke from the back. "Dance for us!"

"What?"

"Dance for us!" she repeated. "Yeh, dance for us!" insisted Orrible Olivia. "Yes, what fun!" yelped Dizzy Debbie. "Then we'll see if we can help you!" offered Clever Clara.

"Ok" agreed Billy, hoping to impress.

Energetic Emily pressed a button on her phone. Music filled the doorway. Billy tried to dance in time with the beat. The girl's faces were desperately trying to hide their smirks. Billy was busting his guts to make all the right moves. Energetic Emily kept changing the music to make it more difficult for him.

"He's rubbish!" shouted Lazy Louise with a yawn.

"Lousy moves dude!" added Clever Clara.

"That's a zero from me!" screamed Dizzy Debbie.

Bashing Bonnie and Orrible Olivia slow clapped and yawned together before running into the house.

"You were really great!" smiled Lying Lilly.

Energetic Emily had a smile all over her face and clapped him.

As the girls disappeared only Energetic Emily and Lying Lilly stayed to speak to Billy.

"Now you have made a complete fool of yourself in front of us, what exactly do you want from us?" asked Lying Lilly.

Billy explained to them all about the cricket match and how they were one player short. Lying Lilly was making hand gestures throughout his little speech. This confused Billy but he felt that he might be making progress so he said nothing. Lying Lilly continued to make hand gestures after he had stopped talking. Energetic Emily didn't utter a word and was making hand gestures back to Lilly.

The two eventually stopped and turned to speak to Billy. "Emily here is your best hope."

"But if you hadn't worked it out already, she is deaf. She says it will not stop her playing cricket though. You must promise me you will be patient with her and help her if she needs it."

Billy had no hesitation in accepting Lying Lilly's terms. "I am sorry she is deaf!" he blurted, straight away realising that he had said something stupid.

"You don't need to be sorry! She isn't (sorry) and it's not your fault!" Lilly continued.

Billy explained how they were training tomorrow. The two girls promised to walk with him to the cricket ground the next day. "We'll knock-on," Lilly uttered. Job done thought Billy. 'Now the team has a glimmer of a chance.'

# Chapter 7

The boys and the girls had made their way to the pavilion on another very cosy morning. A whole gaggle of noisy children. Some tall. Some short. They were already outside of the pavilion. A gangly youth was standing on a picnic table clutching a piece of paper in his hand. Dressed in cricket whites he gestured for Billy, George, Lilly and Emily to join the throbbing throng.

The youth waited as the four found a shady spot tucked just behind an attentive and smiling Sachin. Billy whispered into Sachin's lobes about Energetic Emily being the last piece of the jigsaw for the team. Sachin smiled at Energetic Emily and gave her a thumbs up. The youth standing on the picnic table held his hands out and indicated for the crowd to listen as he placed his palms face down in a wavy movement in front of himself.

The group fell silent as they tuned into the words of the snowy youth.

"Good morning all!"

The crowd responded with a similar greeting.

"My name is Cliff…Cliff Hangar and I am the captain

of the Skaggyness Under-16 team. Thanks to all of you for coming."

"I just want to say that I know we have not beaten Beston in this annual match for many, many years."

"1971!" someone shouted from the crowd of youngsters in front of Cliff.

"Erm…1971…anyway that doesn't mean we will lose this time," Cliff acclaimed totally without conviction.

"It does," piped a voice from the middle of the group of budding players.

"We will be thrashed, we're always thrashed by Beston. Every year, they're too good. They just come here to laugh at us," claimed Kevin Peters in his distinct South African accent that caught the ears of Billy particularly. Being a well- travelled young man himself he thought to himself, 'I have never been to South Africa…yet'.

Cliff was keen to try to quell the words of Kevin and responded meekly.

"It's not the winning it's the taking part."

Sachin was shaking his head in disgust and disappointment. He said nothing but really didn't feel that taking part was enough. He loved the feeling of winning. Sachin bit his lip and reminded himself that he loved the game first and winning second. But he loved cricket so much more when his team won.

A hand went up from the group.

"Yes? What is it?" Cliff enquired.

Morgan Murphy asked of him, "Is the match going ahead because nearly all our first team players have claimed they're on holiday or injured." 'He sounds Irish,' Billy was thinking.

Cliff Hangar gasped before replying, "Yes we do have a lot of players running scared of Beston. The good news everybody here is able to play. We do, at least have a team."

Cliff was nearly sixteen and it would be his last game as captain of the Skaggyness under-16 team. He was, inside of himself, totally convinced that his team would be publicly humiliated. It was only too true that Beston would be arriving with their very best 11 players in the county, if not the country. Skaggyness only had three players who were even 15; himself, Morgan Murphy and Kevin Peters. He looked around at the youngsters in front of him and spotted a baby-faced Sachin and one or two players who he knew to be fourteen years-old.

"We have a team, not necessarily a CRICKET team!" whispered Kevin Peters to Morgan Murphy.

The younger players in the team had arrived with big smiles on their faces. They were so delighted to be asked to play for Skaggyness. Their faces had turned to despair as they sensed their presence was a disappointment to the older players. Cliff gave way to a looming figure and he leaped off the creaking picnic table as coach Joe jumped up.

Coach Joe gave a confident beaming smile which matched the Sun above their baking heads. He quickly echoed the welcome that had already been given to those that would be forming the makeshift side.

Coach Joe lifted the spirits of the players as he claimed there was a route to victory!

"Right now then. Listen carefully. I have some important information about the match. We're going to be playing the new 100 ball format of the game. So make sure you make every ball count. (He gestured to Cliff to handout a piece of paper to all the players with the rules on them.) Make sure you have a read through the rules but essentially it's the same game as always. Yes with less balls in the match and of course five balls in an over."

He waited a moment for Cliff to retake his place so that he had the full attention of the group.

"I am aware that the team is a younger one than usual at this level. I am also aware that for a few of you it is your very first game for Skaggyness. I have also learned that at least three of you have never played organised cricket before, so welcome and thanks to you for your support," the youngsters clapped themselves and the newbies.

"Now …the batting order."

A whirring noise came to the group's attention as a small drone appeared above them. It was clearly interested in their meeting. Coach Joe tried to grab it but it was just out of reach. Kevin grabbed a sweeping brush but as he tried to swat it the drone simply went out of reach. It was not going to move away. Billy said he thought it had a camera on it. Someone was very interested in them.

"Leave it! We'll just have to pretend it's not there," Joe bellowed with frustration. Everybody seemed to shuffle slightly closer to Coach Joe. His waspish build and thick blonde hair seemed to transfix the team as they strained to listen to their own names.

"Openers: Cliff Hangar and Sachin Dulkar."

Cliff smiled and looked admiringly at Sachin who was busying himself with his own grinning. He was already calculating the impact of only having one-hundred balls in an innings.

"Batting three and four; Kevin Peters and Morgan Murphy."

The two named players shook hands with each other.

Coach Joe continued, "Batting five: Kane Taylor and at six Megan Perry."

Those who had heard their name quietly moved to the back of the group to wait for a chance to speak with one another which left a smaller group still straining their ears.

"At seven will be Steve Gilchrist, who will also be wicketkeeper."

Coach Joe quickly finished the list of, "Eight, Stafanie Archer, nine Emily Burton, ten Billy Ranger and eleven George Forest."

Coach Joe smiled and promptly jumped off the table. He strode over to the wall of the pavilion and he pinned the team sheet to the noticeboard. He also pinned a second piece of paper. It was the Beston team.

# Chapter 8

With the drone still hovering above them.

Sachin waved to Lying Lilly, Energetic Emily, George and Billy to come over to the noticeboard.

Emily was first to read the Beston team. Billy caught her up and read the names aloud while asking Sachin if he knew them. After all, cricket was Sachin's creed and he seemed to know so much.

The Beston team read:

Sanath Perera
Brian Holder (Captain)
Virat Sharma
Roy Jason
Heather Taylor
Imad Hafeez
Jhulan Raj
Lisa Brunt
Chris Stokes
Kaf Rabada
Josh Bairstow (Wicket keeper)

Billy was always super inquisitive and badgered Sachin for as much information about the opposition as possible. Sachin explained what he knew about as many of the players as he could. In the main, all Sachin could do was just explain how they were all great players.

"Their captain, Holder, is a giant. He is only fifteen but he is a huge dark mountain. He bowls with the strength of a rhinoceros and the speed of a cheetah!" Sachin explained. They are very strong in their batting line-up. Even their wicket keeper can thrash a ball around super-quick as well as possessing the spring of a gazelle behind the stumps."

"But the girls are rubbish. Right?" Billy looked for affirmation as George quietly listened over Billy's shoulder. As did the drone.

Sachin stepped back and looked shocked at Billy's suggestion. "They have Heather Taylor, England under-16 international, Jhulan Raj is their leading wicket taker and just happens to be the girlfriend of one of my cousins. As for Lisa Brunt, well she played for Yorkshire under-16s before she moved to Beston and in her last match took three-for-six in the last over."

"I don't know what any of that means…" responded Billy; "Or me," quipped George.

"But I get the point that the girls in this team are good players."

Sachin nodded furiously in agreement.

When Sachin stopped admiring every one of the Beston team, he noticed Energetic Emily was signing excitedly to Lying Lilly. Energetic Emily was discussing with her sister the footnote at the bottom of the 100 game format rules given out earlier. It stated that the match, which will begin at 2 p.m. on August Bank Holiday Monday, would be streamed live by the Beston Broadcasting Corporation on UTube, Headbook and Vineo!

After reading that they all took a bit of a gasp. "That means my relations back in India will be watching. My Uncle Ganguly will have made sure the whole of India knows that he intends to humiliate my father to as big an audience as possible!"

"More than that, those streaming platforms guarantee that this match could possibly reach every single country in the modern world!" noted Billy.

"Nobody is going to be bothered about this match outside Skaggyness and Beston, surely" added George.

Sachin added that many of the players on both sides had family connections to other countries. "They have family backgrounds in so many countries: Afghanistan, Australia, Bangladesh, India, Ireland, New Zealand, Pakistan, South Africa, Sri Lanka and the West Indies."

"We have just gone GLOBAL!" exclaimed Billy.

Lying Lilly pointed out that whatever happens in the match tomorrow it could be seen around the world and recorded to be played back over and over again. Billy said he liked the idea of watching his brilliant self. George pointed out that it would also record every dropped ball, every failure to hit the ball and every time someone falls over.

"You could be humiliated for the rest of your life!" shouted George, who dropped to his knees and held his face in his hands.

"I am glad you're showing confidence young George. There's nothing that beats positive thinking," added Lying Lilly.

Cliff Hangar shepherded everybody towards the nets for a final practise before the big day. While glancing at the drone still above them. Coach Joe ran them through some physical exercises and a little guidance on best fielding practice as the morning slipped away. At noon they broke for home. Coach Joe and Captain Cliff had one last word before they left.

Coach Joe reminded everybody that cricket was a sport, always to be played in a sporting manner. Cliff Hangar added that everybody should arrive a full-hour before the two-o'clock start. Kit would be sorted then for those who did not have their own. "I will see you all then." With that the team dispersed; as did the drone.

# CHAPTER 9

It was late Monday morning at the ground. Sachin had already been there for several hours. He was joined by his young peers. Energetic Emily was just completing her fifth circuit of the pitch. Billy had done one circuit and that was enough. George did half a circuit and fell over. He daintily hobbled back to where Sachin was playing keepy-uppy with a white cricket ball and his momentarily chosen bat.

Lying Lilly had chosen to come and hang out; she would be joined by her sisters later. She was already lying in the boiling Sun after showering herself in protective sun cream.

When Energetic Emily eventually stopped, Sachin saw the need for a drink. He grabbed a sponsored cool bag with a dozen bottles of chilled water. They took to the nearest bench by the side of the pitch to find shade and Sachin had advised a slow intake of the liquid.

Billy saw the opportunity to ask some burning questions. "See that white ball you're playing with, is that what we will be using in the match?"

Sachin replied, "It won't be that particular ball but it will be a ball like this."

"I thought we were using a red cricket ball?" continued Billy.

"It is just a colour!" quipped George.

"No, it is a different type of ball. Haven't you heard of red and white ball cricket?" added Sachin.

Together his band of batters responded with a resounding NO!

Energetic Emily had been lip-reading the conversation and was thinking about the heat. She was curious as to the difference between the red and the white ball. They had only ever used plastic balls and tennis balls in school. She asked Sachin to explain the difference.

Sachin took a deep breath before he started his explanation. He found it very frustrating that not everybody had such a passion for cricket and an understanding of the game as he did.

Sachin explained that traditionally cricket did use a red ball. "However, the shorter versions of the game has seen a slightly harder white ball used. It is because the game is being played in floodlights and at night more so a white ball is easier to see."

"Aagh," the group nodded their understanding.

"Can you pass me another bottle of water?" George asked their little cricket teacher. "Me too," added Billy, "It is so, so hot!"

"That's climate change for you!" Energetic Emily interjected.

"No such thing!" bellowed Lying Lilly. "She's always banging on about climate change. There's no such thing just hot, cold and rainy days."

Energetic Emily jumped to her feet. She had recorded many arguments with her sister about climate change.

"I think there is something in it," asserted it Billy.

"I think there is too," agreed George.

Sachin said he would like to know more. "Oh know, that'll just set her off!" warned Lying Lilly.

Energetic Emily insisted Lying Lilly help her explain to the boys some home truths about climate change. She continued and signed to Lilly so she could be her voice, "The Earth's atmosphere now has 411 parts of Carbon Dioxide for every million parts of air. Carbon dioxide is a greenhouse gas. Too much carbon dioxide in the air makes Earth get warmer and warmer. When humans burn fossil fuels, like petrol and coal, carbon dioxide is produced."

The boys were listening and nodding.

Energetic Emily was hard to stop when she was on a roll. She couldn't pass up her opportunity to inform a captive audience.

"The problem doesn't stop there. The Earth's global average temperature has increased by 1.9 degrees Fahrenheit since 1880."

Billy paused for thought a second before suggesting that 1.9 degrees was a tiny amount. His suggestion just seemed to infuriate her.

She progressed her frustration by explaining through

Lilly, "The global average temperature combines the temperatures of all the hot places, all the cold places, and all the places in between. It is a very important measure of changes going on in Earth's machinery. A rise of just one degree Fahrenheit (°F) on a sunny day where you live has little effect. But over the whole Earth, a rise of 1°F makes a big difference. Think! Normally, water at 0°C is solid ice. But water above 0°C is liquid water.

Even a small rise in the Earth's global temperature results in melting ice at the North and South Poles. It means rising seas. It means flooding in some places and drought in others. It means that some plants and animals thrive while others starve. It can mean big changes for humans too. And that's why this number is a very big deal."

Billy was particularly impressed with Energetic Emily. He not only thought it was incredible how much she knew about the subject but just how fantastic it was that she was so passionate about it.

The boys kept their heads down and shifted their position a little awkwardly as Energetic Emily's explanation gathered headway. Sachin thought steam was coming out her ears.

By now Lying Lilly, who had heard it all before, was a little tired and tried to stop her saying anything else. Sachin and George tried to not make eye contact as a clue to her to stop but the boys gave Billy a look as he added fuel to Energetic Emily's fire.

"So what is happening to the ice?"

Energetic Emily smiled as she had just received the

green light to keep her passion at a premium for her captured audience.

"Look what you've done now!" Lying Lilly interrupted speaking for herself.

Energetic Emily gripped her sister's arm to tell her she hadn't finished.

George was getting annoyed with this unexpected lecture, "So what?" he asked her. Billy quickly changed the subject and pointed at the drone which had returned to follow them. "That's just not right!" Billy quickly made a phone call on his mobile. He had rung his dad, an electronics expert, and alerted him to the presence of the drone which had returned. The drone continued to hover. Billy beamed as he came off the phone grinning as he waved at the drone.

"I'm with you," Billy said trying to support Emily and pretending he had been listening to her as she appeared to bring her rants to an end.

George leaned over to Sachin and whispered, "I think he's in love."

As the two boys giggled Lying Lilly advised her sister to calm down as she had to save her anger up for the match. Sachin stood-up and suggested they should have some of the sandwiches and samosas that had been prepared and left for the team in the changing room. It would be time for action on the pitch before long. He also reminded them all to make sure they smothered themselves in sun protection cream just as Lying Lilly had already done. "Way ahead of you!" Billy said as he already taken all precautions to stay Sun Safe.

# Chapter 10

Monday afternoon came before the Sun could decide how strong to be that day. The group of super nervous and super eager budding cricket superstars of Skaggyness were now joined by their older team mates. They were quiet but mischievous. Sachin helped Billy and George to find kit to fit from deep within the dingy, stink laden changing room the team were gathered in. Energetic Emily had sorted herself out and was already sitting down, calming down, looking pensive and ready for action.

Sachin was nervous as well but he always dealt with his nerves by doing things. He had been up out of his bed since six o'clock that morning. He had been watching old UTube clips from the World Cup to get his mind focused. Sachin had been briefly pretending to lift the World Cup after smacking a six off the final ball. He had lifted one of his treasured bats to the window and took his acclaim from the imagined delirious crowd of admirers.

He had not wanted to see or talk to his father that morning. He had decided that his dad's obsession with his Uncle was not his problem. He did not need to hear, yet again, how crucial it was to defeat his Uncle Ganguly and the reasons why there was such venomous blood between the two men. He was desperate to win every cricket match, whoever the opposition, but he knew his dad would be heaping expectation on him at breakfast and he did not need that!

Sachin had quickly grabbed some fruit and a carton of milk. He showered and grabbed his kit, including his treasured bats before slipping out. His family had been successfully avoided as he took a slow stroll to the ground arriving almost two hours before Coach Joe. Coach Joe was quite used to Sachin waiting on him to open-up. Today had been no different to exactly what he had come to expect from young Sachin. He would be hanging around for hours before the match but he just loved to see and smell the ground before he got started.

Sachin had taken Billy, George and Emily under his wing. For these guys, Sachin was their Captain so Cliff Hangar was relaying any messages to these three players through him.

Energetic Emily was constantly changing the position she sat in and was tidying and re-tidying everything in sight as the minutes counted themselves down. George was just blathering away and Billy told him he had verbal diarrhoea. George had been to the toilet three-times in the last half-an-hour. He kept muttering to himself, "We're going to be humiliated around the world."

Billy was also nervous and was busy eating everything

in sight. "Can I have that apple? Do you want that piece of chocolate? Are you eating that Scotch Egg?" His requests had met with varying success but it was giving him something to do.

Along with the Captain, Kevin Peters and Morgan Murphy were the oldest players. The two of them were dominating the changing room by bowling a soft ball to each other. They switched the batting position between themselves after every ten balls to help get them in the right frame of mind for their first 100 game.

The other players were spread around the room some talking, some staying hushed all of them following or developing their pre-match routines. Coach Joe was smiling as he spent all the time on his phone talking to seemingly anyone who had a number in his phone. His constant smiling was helping to relax most people who caught sight of it.

Lying Lilly popped her head around the door to wish her sister good luck. Energetic Emily jumped up and bolted across the floor to talk to her. Lilly signed a message to her and Emily was heard to respond, "Brilliant!" Emily turned to say to the rest of the team that there was several hundred people here to watch.

Win, lose or draw some people love an audience. The bigger the crowd, the bigger the performance was what Coach Joe had always told Sachin.

The final detail in the team's preparation came when Coach Joe announced they had been given new shirts to wear. He explained that their old red tracksuit bottoms would have to do. He placed a pile of brand new navy blue cotton t-shirts on the table in the dressing room.

"There all the same size," observed Kevin Peters.

Kevin started to throw the shirts around the room shouting at each player as he aimed for them. The t-shirts were all adult medium. This was fine for the older players but they looked rather odd and incredibly roomy on the younger, smaller children.

Sachin looked around the room, collecting his thoughts. "At least we look like a team, of sorts," noted Cliff Hangar.

The noose of time was closing in. "The knives are being sharpened for you Cliff," Kevin Peters offered no comfort for his Captain. Kevin used to be Captain but after zero wins in any match, in any form of the game, he decided to quit as there was simply no personal glory in the position. It left him no one to blame when the team lost.

The door opened and the sunlight entered the dimly lit room. A dark figure asked for the captain to come for the coin toss.

At precisely 1.45 pm Cliff Hangar walked out of the changing room. Brian Holder, the Beston Captain, was simultaneously leaving their changing room. They met in the middle of the pitch and were greeted by two people in white coats and hats. "I am Isaac Mthuru-Bailey and this is Sarah Heyhoe-Flint. We are your match umpires." They all stopped for a moment and looked towards the heavens. The drone was back and was following their every move.

Brian Holder stood square-on to Cliff as he slowly lowered his head as to make eye-contact with the Skaggyness Captain. As he did so, his giant frame cast a chilling shadow that seemed to punch Cliff's shadow out of sight. Cliff had gone cold as he was momentarily hidden from the incredible summer heat.

The two Captains shook hands. Seconds later, Brian Holder let Master Hangar have his hand back after he had crushed it enough to cause Cliff pain that produced a small tear in his left-eye. Cliff was desperately trying to hide the damage that had just been inflicted on him.

Sarah Heyhoe-Flint stepped forward and asked the away team captain to call the toss. "Heads," he stated.

"Heads it is," she informed them both.

"We'll bat," Brian Holder told them.

"See you back out here in ten minutes," Isaac Mthuru-Bailey instructed.

# CHAPTER 11

The crowd were gathering. They were waiting for the two teams. Lying Lilly was still sun bathing. She was glued to a screen with her ear pods on. She was monitoring what was being said on the exciting live broadcast on UTube.

The commentary was so…

"For Skaggyness and Beston the time is very much now!" announced Mithali Goswami, who was a very slick presenter.

"Since 1971 this match has witnessed some great players from Beston to go on to play for both their counties and their countries. Skaggyness have only a single victory to their name as it has always been Beston producing great future international cricketers."

She handed over to her co-presenter, Phil Agnew, "Hello and welcome to Skaggyness as we're here for the climax of the under-16 cricket season. We have had an incredible summer of action and Beston arrive here undefeated in all competitions. They have smashed an incredible two-hundred sixes and four-hundred fours in that time.

This final challenge of the season will guarantee more of that from the Beston players. We are hugely looking forward to seeing the wonderful batting of the likes of Virat Sharma, Sanath Perera, Roy Jason and Heather Taylor. We will be watching some the countries top young players in the field with Josh Bairstow behind the stumps and leading catcher Imad Hafeez. Beston also boast the fastest player in the field in Kaf Rabada."

"Who are you most looking forward to seeing Mithali?"

"Well Phil, I am looking forward to seeing Heather Taylor leading female batter this season anywhere in the country. Of course in a similar way Lisa Brunt leading female bowler. Not to forget the Beston captain Brian Holder a fearsome sight for any player."

"Thanks Mithali, I'm particularly excited to watch Chris Stokes today, dangerous with bat and ball perhaps the most exciting all-rounder in the UK."

"Now there is a real sense of anticipation here in Skaggyness. The crowd have arrived here in their droves and sunhats. There is a buzz of excitement for this end of season one-hundred ball challenge. They play for the Olympic Hypermarket Shield, a trophy Beston have won annually since Skaggyness's only victory in 1971.

Sana explained, "Beston have won the toss and elected to bat first. It is far from overcast conditions. The Sun has been baking the ground since first light so it might be a struggle for the Skaggyness opening bowlers in the first phase of the game."

Skaggyness slowly emerged from their dressing room. They were greeted by nervous applause. 'Go smack 'em boys …er and girls' a voice cried out. Cliff Hangar was politely instructing all the players where to field. Energetic Emily, Billy and George had to be escorted to their areas in which the captain wanted them to field. The crowd was tittering in the raging furnace of a pitch at the seemingly clueless wonders that had took to the field. George simply looked bemused. He was desperately hoping someone would shout at him when he needed to do something.

Cliff took up a position close to the wicketkeeper behind the stumps, acting as a slip fielder. The umpires were keenly observed having a close-up chat with Captain Cliff. They were explaining that in the one-hundred ball format the first twenty-five balls were a powerplay. The powerplay meant that Cliff Hangar had to set his field with only two players outside the marked area, which had a thirty-yard (around 27.5 m) circumference from the centre of the pitch.

When the players were all set, the umpires handed Stafanie Archer the white ball and reminded her and the Skaggyness captain they could bowl only a maximum of twenty balls for each bowler. Each bowler would be instructed by the captain whether he wanted them to bowl in a group of five-balls or ten-balls.

"Just five Staf," Cliff was heard to instruct her as she quickly went through a warm-up routine.

So many of the gathering crowd were also watching and listening on their phones and tablets. They were busy taking photos and everybody seemed to be claiming a close relationship with at least one player in one of the teams.

Stafanie, was a right armed fast (for a teenager) bowler and she was moving like an antelope as she was about to release the first ball.

# CHAPTER 12

The crowd was listening for the pins dropping as Stafanie thundered down the wicket. A single-minded set of eyes peered from inside a helmet searching for the orbiting white spot.

Phil Agnew noted, "It'll be Taylor to Perera for the opening ball."

The ball flew wildly down the wicket. "It'll be a wide. Perera had a good look at the ball as it went passed. First ball down the wicket and that is a great show of intent from Archer.

1 ball gone. Beston: 1 run for 0 wickets.

As the game continued the crowd and players of both sides were abuzz. They weren't just chatting about the game were busily explaining the rules of the competition to one-another.

"And that spurted away through gully and it will hurry away for 4. The outfield is always quick at Skaggyness," – Mithali commented.

2 balls gone. Beston: 5 runs for 0 wickets.

Phil Agnew excitedly noted, "That's close. Nipping back, it's given. Perera leg before wicket (lbw).

3 balls gone. Beston: 5 runs for 1 wicket.

Mithali Goswama and Phil Agnew were excelling over the expected performances of the Beston players. With only 100 balls per team, Phil suggested it was vital each side made every ball count.

As Perera exited the field, Virat Sharma joined the Beston captain Brian Holder at the sharp end.

Archer was starting to feel the heat. The blazing heat from the Sun coupled with the scorching heat from the Beston batters.

40 balls gone. Beston: 79 runs for 1 wicket.

The umpires suggested a drinks break after the next ten-balls. Cliff Hangar had to try something. Beston were getting away from Skaggyness. He was already thinking that it would be near impossible to catch them if the scoring rate continued at almost two-per ball. Coach Joe could only shrug his shoulders as Cliff looked at him for inspiration. Sweat was wiped and examined in his hand. Perhaps the perspiration will hold the answer. He looked around his team for his fifth bowler. The drone continued to hover over Skaggyness players. It made concentration difficult for them. It appeared to keep its distance from Beston players.

The first four had all bowled half of their allotted balls. He beckoned to Kevin Peters to take a turn. Peters turned away from him. The South African stubbornness, that was so often Kevin's friend, had visited him again today. Again Cliff Hangar waved for KP to bowl. Peters didn't seem remotely interested in responding to his captain.

Hangar tried and tried again. KP walked away in the opposite direction. He appeared to take a phone out of his pocket. Kevin Peters decided that this was a good moment to send a text or two; just when his team and his captain needed his support.

"That's odd," noted Mrs. Dulkar, Sachin's mum, who was knitting on the front row as Mr. Dulkar was about to bellow. She stopped him from interfering by giving him a sharp jab with a blunt knitting needle. "He's just a boy," she suggested. "He's a disgrace! Ignoring his captain! What's that about?" retorted Mr. Dulkar.

Mr. Dulkar shouted to Cliff, "Sachin can bowl you know. He's not just a batsman."

It caught Cliff's attention. He didn't see anyone else stepping up. He called Sachin over. He really didn't want to ask the younger players to do anything. Reluctantly he asked Sachin, "Can you bowl?"

# CHAPTER 13

Sachin gave his captain a little nod. Cliff was desperate. Cliff knew that Sachin was a keen cricketer. He knew that Sachin was raved about by coaches, a little master of the art of batting; at least for his age.

"Oh well," sighed Cliff somewhat submissively, as he tossed the ball to his last hope.

"We are being well and truly smacked about. Just bowl the best you can," he instructed.

Sachin nodded. Although bowling wasn't what he was best at, he was keen to test out these 'brilliant' Beston batters.

While there was a natural break in the play, George, who was fielding out on the boundary close to Billy, ran over to him.

"Billy mate, what's the score?"

"I think they've scored quite a lot of runs."

"But they've lost three wickets," George suggested.

"No, they haven't. No one's been out since the first few balls," insisted Billy.

George pondered this. "You're out if you're caught though and I have seen three catches."

Billy helped him out, "Yes. But they've all been by spectators while they've been scoring sixes!"

"Gotcha!" and with that George scurried back to his place.

Sachin went to have a word with Billy. The crowd could see Sachin gesturing and pointing at the drone above his head. Billy turned to shout to his dad. His dad, an expert in electronics, had promised Billy he would take care of the drone. Sachin urged Billy that he needed it gone.

Billy's dad saluted his son as Billy gave him a signal. "My dad wants you to stand next to the pavilion wall." Sachin wandered back to the umpires. He told them that he was a little sick and needed to get some air into him. He told them that he just needed to walk to and from the pavilion then he would be ok. "Highly irregular!" they both commented, but let him walk anyway. The drone followed him everywhere he went. At one point, flew low enough to scrape his head. The drone was now clearly targeting Sachin.

As he stood by the wall of the pavilion, Billy's dad started up his own drone. A monster drone in the shape of a square block. It was five times the size of the drone bugging Sachin. The drone rocketed through the air and was heading towards Sachin's head. Sachin knew it was coming and he ducked to tie his laces a second before it would have collided with his head. As he bent down it missed him and smashed into the 'bugging' drone splattering it all over the wall.

Both drones fell to the ground. Sachin casually strolled back to his position to resume the match. "Cheers dad!" shouted Billy. Billy's dad was dancing a dad dance, both arms waving about with the odd dab as a celebration of his accurate targeting.

The crowd was growing as the afternoon ticked. They were muttering as they nudged each other at the picked out the slight figure of a fresh faced Sachin warming-up to bowl.

Mr and Mrs Dulkar were overwrought, shuffling in their seats. At this moment Mr. Dulkar glimpsed his nemesis. "Sunil Ganguly!" he cried.

Sunil Ganguly was laughing. "You losers have lost again! Already they're sending your runt of a child!" as he lobbed a verbal grenade at Mr. Dulkar.

"You…! Dare call my boy that! You…You…" Mr. Dulkar was searching for his words, stammering as he was trying to halt a charge from his anger.

He stood up and he came within a metre of Ganguly. The crowd had noticed the two men stand-up and move towards each other. Sachin and all the players had noticed too.

Ganguly was beckoning aggressively to Mr. Dulkar with his two arms to come to him.

Mr. Dulkar was bellowing, "You think you are such a tough man don't you but you are just a little boy!"

"Well Dulkar, you have intellect below monkey!"

They continued to blast each other.

"And you Gangoonie, you think you're such a big dog but you are a little tiny kitten."

"Yes, well my father went to medical school and yours went to the school of rickshaw!"

"Your mama looks like a crab's backside!"

Ganguly tells Mr. Dulkar, "Your very existence is a waste of time!"

As the crowd watched. Sachin shook his head; part in shame, part in anger and part in frustration.

The two were pulled away from each other with one last parting shot.

Ganguly shouted he would see him later to laugh at the size of the defeat for Skaggyness.

Mr. Dulkar retorted by bawling he would stuff the biggest bhaji he could find where his shadow can film the pain for him. He was really proud of that one!

Sachin was waiting for the spat to die down. He just wanted to play cricket. But this scene was one he had grown used to all his life. He always had to suppress his anger when his dad was being attacked.

Umpire Heyhoe-Flint indicated that they were ready to restart, when silence had emerged beyond the boundary once more.

# CHAPTER 14

Sachin didn't need a long run-up to bowl a cricket ball. A bowler has two main roles. The first is to try and limit the batter's scoring and the other is to try and take wickets. In the 100 ball game both can be vital but stopping them scoring is huge.

On UTube the commentators had been entertained by the family sideshow. "Now we can see what this young lad Sachin has got. I suggest more fours and sixes for Beston," predicted Phil Agnew.

Sachin began his bowl. Mithali Goswami noted, "He clearly has a nice smooth rhythmical approach to the wicket."

The ball twizzled in the air and seem to float towards Brian Holder who stepped forward. He launched his body into a full swing the moment the ball was in reach. "Thwack!"

"That's away back over the bowler's head and it's a massive six!" enthused Goswami.

41 balls gone. Beston: 85 runs for 1 wicket.

"I think the decision to ask this boy to bowl is a little cruel," Agnew stated.

Undeterred, Sachin shook himself and went again.

"Smooth approach once again, flight of the ball slightly lower this time…Holder gets hold of it again. And it races away as the umpire puts her arm across her chest to signal four runs."

42 balls gone. Beston: 89 runs for 1 wicket.

Sachin took a look at the huge frame of Brian Holder. He adjusted the position of his approach to the wicket. He let the ball go with a slightly quicker step into the run-up. Holder left the ball and the umpire raised her arms wide apart. A wide had been signalled. Cliff Hangar was shaking his head. Kevin Peters was laughing his head-off.

42 balls gone. Beston: 90 runs for 1 wicket.

Holder showed Sachin as many of his pearly whites as possible as the two made eye contact. Sachin went again.

"And that's four more, this time over cover point,"

43 balls gone. Beston: 94 runs for 1 wicket.

It was exactly the same result for the next two balls. Surely Cliff Hangar would put the bowler out of his misery?

45 balls gone. Beston: 102 runs for 1 wicket.

Cliff went over to talk to Sachin. Sachin wanted to bowl five more straight away. "Nobody else has Sachin."

"Nobody else is me!" Sachin protested confidently.

Cliff had no other plan.

"Go for it!"

This time he was bowling to Virat Sharma.

Sachin's body language appeared confident despite the battering he had taken so far. All the Skaggyness players smiled and lifted their spirits slightly as Sachin was happy to bowl again.

He bowled his sixth ball and Sharma smacked him for six runs over deep-square leg.

Sachin took a long look at Sharma. He then went to Cliff Hangar to have a word.

Cliff indicated to the fielders on the boundary to step forward a few steps.

Sachin began his approach.

"Here the boy comes again, this time he has gone over the wicket it is a good one. Sharma meets it and it is gone high in the air and looks like another six. Oh it might be short, the fielders under it. It's taken. Virat Sharma's out! Caught by one Emily Burton."

"Yes!" was a cry from the whole Skaggyness team as Energetic Emily had taken the catch, visibly lifting the whole team. Maybe the mountain was already too high for Skaggyness to climb.

47 balls gone. Beston: 108 runs for 2 wickets.

Beston didn't look too bothered. Mr and Mrs Dulkar were as proud as punch as Mr Dulkar was busy telling everybody, "That's my boy!"

Sachin had to bowl to Roy Jason next. Roy Jason was the highest run scorer this season for Beston. The commentators were busy spelling out just how good this guy was.

"From his last seven innings he has scored 808 runs."

"You're absolutely right Phil. An impressive strike rate of 115.43."

"What will he do to young Sachin?"

Sachin bowled him a yorker. He then bowled him another yorker, followed by a slow short ball. Roy couldn't get near any of them.

50 balls gone. Beston: 108 runs for 2 wickets.

Cliff Hangar was again looking around for his next bowler. He checked his options.

(Each bowler can bowl a maximum of twenty balls.)

| Bowler | Balls | Runs | Wickets |
| --- | --- | --- | --- |
| Hangar | 10 | 23 | – |
| Archer | 15 | 28 | 1 |
| Perry | 15 | 28 | – |
| Dulkar | 10 | 9 | 1 |

He did not have many options. Nobody was keen to bowl. Nobody wanted to get smashed all over the place and have it watched by friends, family and who knows!

He took the next five himself and Archer and Perry the next ten.

After 65 balls, the scorecard made for grim reading.

Beston: 153 for 2.

Sachin suggested to Cliff that if the older lads did not want to bowl he should give Emily a go. Sachin insisted that she was very quick and they will not have seen her bowl before. Cliff gave it a go. "I'll take the next five then she's on tell her."

Energetic Emily was delighted for the opportunity.

Beston: 70 balls gone. 165 for 2.

She took the ball and gave it a thorough wipe on her trousers. "That's the deaf girl," the crowd were heard to comment. Lying Lilly was now bolt upright looking around to see if any of her sisters were somewhere about to watch their Energetic Emily take a bowl.

"Well, who's this Mathali?" enquired Phil Agnew.

"According to the team list, it is a young girl playing in her very first match for Skaggyness; Emily Burton."

She began her run-up. Cliff trusted Sachin's judgement. Sachin actually had no idea if Emily could bowl or not but she had been so intense he was convinced this match meant something to her. He gambled she would be good.

The umpire was looking closely at her feet on approach. The umpires have to check the delivery of the ball is legal. As she approached the wicket she took-off from the non-bowling foot (her right foot as she was a left-arm bowler). She landed on her opposite foot (her left foot), her arm raised and her head still, looking right at the stumps.

As her front foot hit the ground she brought her right-arm over, keeping it arrow like, then releasing the ball with perfect timing. Her head was upright, target still in sight.

As she released her missile her body kept moving towards the target. The ball in flight was deceptively fast. It flew passed a vacant looking Brian Holder and then exploded on impact with middle stump!

The whole crowd heard the middle stick snap, except

Emily. She looked at her handy work and was quickly mobbed by her team mates.

Beston: 71 balls gone: 165 for 3.

As Holder left the field he passed a comment to his replacement Heather Taylor. "That was a fluke. There's no way she will be as fast again."

Heather was laughing as she adjusted the chin strap on her helmet.

Energetic Emily bowled four more balls.

Heather Taylor could not get her bat on the ball.

Beston: 75 balls gone: 165 for 3.

Cliff was thinking about the last 25 balls. He suddenly felt slightly better about his choices. He asked Sachin for his thoughts as everyone else seemed to have deserted him as the leader. Sachin suggested Emily should stay on for another five, he should bowl the next ten himself and leave Emily the last ten. Cliff was happy with that.

Energetic Emily and Sachin bowled sixteen dot balls (a ball in which no run is scored off or wicket taken) between them, before the end of the Beston innings.

Beston: 100 balls gone: 174 for 3.

The two sides returned to the pavilion for the break and tea! "Cake time!" shouted Billy.

# CHAPTER 15

The moment the Skaggyness team went back into the pavilion, a row quickly broke out. Kevin Peters rounded on Cliff Hangar. He suggested the team was now being run by infants!

Coach Joe intervened and tried to calm the players down. The team listened closely to Coach Joe. He was really full of praise for everyone who just kept toiling away in the heat.

"It's hard out there in the heat so freshen-up your sun lotion and take on plenty of water," he accentuated on the need for fluids. Peters was writing off their chances. He suggested that scoring nearly two off every ball was impossible for THIS team against THAT team! Morgan Murphy suggested he could score fours and sixes off every ball he faced so he suggested to them they should relax.

Coach Joe asked if he could just have a quick word. He suggested to Cliff that he went down the corridor and knock on the door of 'The Green Room'. This was where the ex- senior players of Skaggyness C.C. gathered. Cliff wondered who might be there.

As he walked down the corridor he reflected on what little sleep he had the night before. He feared a thrashing and despite the best efforts of some, a thrashing is what they were getting. As he approached The Green Room he had heard Coach Joe talk about the secrets this room kept and he had never had the opportunity to go in.

He could hear a piano playing behind the green door of the green room. He could hear laughing behind the green door. It was a big moment getting in there, a real honour. He wondered who was there and what he would see.

He knocked once, and he tried to tell them he'd been there. The door slammed, he noted that hospitality was thin there. He wondered, "Just what's going on in there?"

He saw an eyeball peeping through a smokey cloud behind the green door. When he said "Joe sent me," someone laughed out loud behind the green door. He frustratingly thought, "All I want to do is join the happy crowd behind the green door."

"Green door, what's that secret you're keeping?"

He made his way back to take his place with his team as it was their turn to bat.

# CHAPTER 16

Mithali Goswami, "Welcome back after this short turnaround."

"Yes, Beston will be keen to display their great array of bowling talent as they look to finish-off their opponents in this curious annual fixture," added Phil Agnew.

Cliff Hangar strode out following the sprinting Beston team. Side-by-side with his rather shorter batting partner. He carried his helmet and switched his carrying hand for it as he paraded to the wicket. He angled his head down to speak to Sachin who was quiet and pensive on his walk. "Now, I know you're going to be nervous young Sachin but remember you are under no pressure. We're not really expected to win you know. They are a great team."

"We're going to win!" insisted Sachin.

Cliff smiled at him and replied, "I know you'd like to think that but you mustn't be too disappointed if it doesn't go our way. They are a brilliant team."

Sachin grimaced as he reiterated, "We're going to win!"

The two umpires took up their positions before

speaking to Cliff Hangar about restarting. Cliff Hangar suggested to the umpires that they should remember that Sachin was a few years younger and that they should watch for aggressive bowling towards him.

The two umpires explained he would get the same rulings and treatments as every other player.

Kaf Rabada was going through a warm-up as he prepared to deliver the first ball of the Skaggyness innings.

Cliff took his usual stance and watched as Rabada began his run towards him. The ball went shooting past him. Cliff played and missed.

Cliff couldn't connect with any of the first five balls.

Score: Skaggyness 0 from 5.

Beston lead by 174 runs.

As the teams changed ends Cliff and Sachin spoke. "We have to score quickly," suggested Sachin.

"Oh, we're okay, we haven't lost a wicket," Cliff highlighted. Sachin was perplexed.

Sachin was to face the next ball.

It was Rabada again and Sachin stared right at him as he came charging down the wicket, snorting like an elephant in a stampede.

Sachin had already noted from his first five balls that Kaf Rabada had great control over the line and length of the ball. He anticipated where his first ball would fall. He wasn't wrong. Sachin pushed his bat towards the ball and met it on the half-volley. The ball flew to the boundary for four runs.

The next ball was identical and this time Sachin angled his bat to gain more lift and drove the ball way up in the air. He then watched it plonk over the boundary for six!

The crowd stood up and cheered. His dad was super excited, "That's my boy! That's my boy!" he bellowed.

Sachin was convinced that Rabada wouldn't give him another ball the same. He adjusted his stance and as the next ball came in he kept still. He placed his bat straight, to meet it on the rise and it killed the power of the ball. He defended the next two balls in a similarly assured fashion.

Score: Skaggyness 10 for 0 from 10 balls.

"That was lovely play young Sachin," Cliff complimented.

"We need runs, lots and quickly," Sachin urged his captain.

Cliff Hangar simply responded with, "All in good time,"

Chris Stokes took up the bowling. He gave Cliff Hangar a chance to get his bat on ball. "Yes!" Cliff shouted. Sachin and Cliff crossed over to gain a run. Sachin connected with the next ball and they crossed once more.

Stokes bowled his next one very central to the wicket. Cliff Hangar played and missed his shot. The Skaggyness captain immediately dropped his head as he heard his middle stump disappear. He didn't look anywhere but at the floor as he took off his gloves and helmet. He tucked his bat under his arm as he walked off.

Score: Skaggyness 12 for 1 from 13 balls.

# CHAPTER 16

As Cliff Hangar exited the field of play he was bumped into by the entering Kevin Peters.

"Sorry," said a smiling Peters.

As Kevin Peters prepared to bat he ran up to Sachin and said, "Leave it to me, just run when I tell you!"

Sachin was motionless in response.

As Chris Stokes bowled his next two balls, Kevin Peters said thanks by taking a four and a single.

Score: Skaggyness 17 for 1 from 15 balls.

"It is clear that Kevin Peters is possibly the best hope Skaggyness have of getting close to the Beston score," remarked Phil Agnew.

As Kevin worked to keep strike, he quickly clocked up a number of runs.

Mithali Goswami noted, "What I like about Kevin's style is his ability to attack every ball."

Sachin ran when he was told to run and worked with Peters so that Kevin could keep strike.

"I hope you're watching kid, I'll show you how to do it!" Peters instructed Sachin.

Score: Skaggyness 43 for 1 from 40 balls.

As KP prepared to launch the ball once again towards the boundary he smiled as he was beaten by a singing ball that he misjudged. The ball hit the edge of his bat and floated right into the hands of the wicket keeper Josh Bairstow.

As he walked off the field he took a quick glance at the scoreboard placed at the opposite end of the pavilion.

K. Peters c Bairstow b Brunt 20

He took a swiping look at a smiling Lisa Brunt, "Ta da hero!" she voiced his way.

Score: Skaggyness 43 for 2 from 41 balls.

The Sun continued to bake the players and the crowd as the umpires insisted on a drinks break for all. It gave Sachin a chance to chat to the incoming Morgan Murphy. Morgan suggested that he should do exactly what KP was doing. Sachin simply added, "Just get runs."

Morgan Murphy slashed away at every ball he faced as soon as the match resumed.

He notched more than one six and told Sachin when he was running.

"Yes!" came a familiar shout and Sachin whizzed to the opposite end of the wicket.

"Yes," Morgan cried as he dashed for a second. "No," Sachin cried. But it was too late.

A super throw from Virat Sharma saw Bairstow run out Murphy, as Sachin made safe.

Score: Skaggyness 86 for 3 from 65 balls. Beston lead by 88 runs with 35 balls to go.

The crowd were boiling. They were discussing the fact

the game was seemingly over and Beston to all appearances had already won.

The next five balls said au revoir to Kane Taylor and adios to Megan Perry. The umpires instructed another drinks break. The crowd were trying to work out the maths of the game. Most had resigned themselves to a Beston win. The Beston players were already planning their celebrations.

Steve Gilchrist strutted out and joined in with the crowd as they examined the scoreboard together.

| Skaggyness | | | |
|---|---|---|---|
| C.Hangar | | b Rabada | 0 |
| S.Dulkar | not out | | 27 |
| K.Peters | c Bairstow | b Brunt | 20 |
| M.Murphy | run out | | 39 |
| K.Taylor | c Hafeez | b Brunt | 0 |
| M.Perry | c Bairstow | b Raj | 0 |
| S.Gilchrist | | | |
| S.Archer | | | |
| E.Burton | | | |
| B.Ranger | | | |
| G.Forest | | | |
| Total | | 86 for 5 from 70 balls | |

"We've no chance now," Gilchrist suggested to Sachin as he greeted him on the field.

"We have 30 balls remaining. We need to score 3 off every ball to win," Sachin maintained.

"The way they bowl? We've no chance," Gilchrist sounded desponded.

Gilchrist scored a four before being out next ball to a slower delivery from Jhulan Raj which completely foxed him. A similar story played out for Archer. This left only the four bambinos of the team left. "We're going to win!" was Sachin's adamant attitude that greeted Energetic Emily as she joined him at the field.

Score: Skaggyness 94 for 7 from 75 balls. Beston lead by 80 with 25 balls remaining.

Energetic Emily smiled warmly as she saw her batting partner's determination. She had watched Sachin outlast six 'superior', older players. He was not out and had slowly collected his runs. 'I will run when you tell me,' Emily smiled her message to him.

The umpires insisted on a drinks break as the heat fried some and poached the others; Sachin plotted a strategy not to get scrambled.

He started to work out factors such as run rate (the number of runs a team is scoring per over), what bowlers were left to bowl, and how the pitch was playing.

# Chapter 17

At the interval Sachin and Energetic Emily took on as much fluid as possible. Sachin was arranging a hand-signal for the two of them to combat Emily's limitation.

As the match resumed, Sachin was surveying the pitch intensely. He zoned in on exactly where all the fielders had been placed. He was busily checking the condition of the pitch. He was trying to carefully judge how it will play and whether it would benefit a particular shot. He knew by his calculations that the two of them, however fast he and Emily might have been, had to try for boundaries to get anywhere near the Beston total. After making a judgement, Sachin bolted over to the umpires and made a request to change his bat. He switched it for a slightly heavier bat.

Sachin went through a series of motions with his new bat. He took a few air swings and checked he could get an effective backswing. While the Beston players sniggered at this young expert, Sachin moved his bat quickly through the air demonstrating his straight and cross-bat shots with just one hand.

The umpires indicated that they must get back to the game. Sachin took a glance over to his parents. His Dad was clapping excitedly shuffling in his seat declaring to all around him that his boy was 'in the zone'.

Hush floated down. And as it settled, a booming voice directed his words at peacock Dulkar, "The only zone your boy is in is the one where he catches a bus back to the pavilion!"

"Ganguly… you're not funny!" came the response.

"Your boy has snot for a brain!" continued Ganguly.

"Don't tell me that is snot funny!" the crowd laughed at the sideshow.

Mrs. Dulkar put her knitting down and held her husband with two arms trying to restrain him from attacking Ganguly.

Sachin simply smiled as he took strike and with peregrine falcon eyes he began his hunt for prey.

The first ball came down like a rocket and Sachin could get nowhere near it. Umpire Mthuru-Bailey lifted both arms up to his shoulders; signalling a wide ball-one run. 'Good start' thought Sachin.

As Jhulan Raj released a missile in his direction, Sachin stepped forward to meet it. When the bat made contact with the ball it was sent skywards. The Beston fielders lost sight of it in the scorching Sun. It was up there so long it had donned a hat and sunglasses by the time it came down over the boundary; just behind a diving Ganguly in the crowd.

With two arms aloft, umpire Heyhoe-Flint watched six-runs effect the scoreboard.

Score: Skaggyness 101 for 7 from 76 balls. Beston lead by 73 runs with 24 balls remaining.

Sachin looked as though he had cut the ball in two as he swept the ball behind him and saw it run passed third man and over the rope. He followed it with a gentle tap to the on side and he and Emily showed their speed as they snatched two. He then edged a shot to the off side where he snatched a single to keep the strike, the Beston fielders clashed as they went to throw the ball. From a panicked over throw, Energetic Emily and her little master ran two more. Raj delivered him an unplayable for her final ball.

The two pitch runners were smiling broadly as they took a check on the score.

Score: Skaggyness 110 for 7 from 80 balls. Beston lead by 64 runs with 20 balls remaining.

"This is a wonderful little cameo by young Dulkar. It will end with treasured but losing runs as Beston are taking a little longer than expected to close this match," commented Mithali Goswami.

The next ball whizzed around Sachin's ears but somehow he made contact with his bat. Sachin feared the worst as he saw the ball floating in the air. It was heading for the Sun. As the ball about turned, it headed on a downward path unseen. It was missed as it came into view, by two fielders who were forced to watch it land just over the boundary. SIX!

"Well that was streaky but you kind of make your own luck sometimes," remarked Phil Agnew. Sachin knew his team were close to defeat and so kept a constant check on the score.

Score: Skaggyness 116 for 7 from 81 balls. Beston lead by 58 runs with 19 balls remaining.

For the next four balls Sachin kept the strike. They darted between the wickets like greyhounds with their tongues basking in the ever relentless sun.

Sachin hit two fours and took a single. Now Energetic Emily met Sachin in the middle of the wicket. She pointed to the scoreboard.

Score: Skaggyness 125 for 7 from 85 balls. Beston lead by 49 runs with 15 balls remaining.

"I do not understand the scoring in this game," Emily made clear to him.

Sachin smirked, it wasn't the first time that he had heard someone say they didn't get the scoring system in a cricket match. Sachin explained the score to her. Emily paused before saying anything in response to him. "How do I help us win? We can win, can't we?"

Sachin replied, "Of course but we need to keep running and thinking about our shots."

Emily insisted that she worked with him to keep him on strike. She thought Sachin's batting was their best hope of a victory. Sachin was delighted with his running mate. He assured her that they could do it!

Sachin knew that to score 49 off 15 balls was asking for a miracle against such a great team. Sachin loved a challenge; bring it on!

Phil Agnew noted to his viewers, "I genuinely

think that this lucky young boy thinks he can win this match."

"Against this Beston team? With their bowlers? He has ridden his luck so far but one great ball or a little mistake and he is gone! Or if Beston can get at the other kids at the crease we will get the expected Beston victory. We can then discuss how many of the Beston players look like future international players," proposed Mithali Goswami.

Sachin had taken up his stance at the crease once more watching hawk-like at bowler Lisa Brunt. As she started her run Sachin signalled to Emily to be ready. Lisa Brunt bowled him a yorker, at which Sachin shifted his feet as if dancing on hot sand and he clipped the ball to the on side for four more.

The next ball produced the same result. Brunt then decided to bowl from the other side of the wicket. As the ball bounced it pinged back up in the air to his chest. Sachin had to twizzle, like a ballerina, to hook the ball around behind square leg. It soared in the air seemingly flying like a ballistic missile directly over Imad Hafeez's head; into the crowd for six!

As Brunt stood with hands on hips glaring at Sachin, he grinned back at her. He knew the next ball would be another danger, he quickly tried to check the score.

Score: Skaggyness 139 for 7 from 88 balls. Beston lead by 35 runs with 12 balls remaining.

Brunt bowled the next ball in exactly the same place but even faster leaving the ball to bounce even higher. It flew over his head and over the wicket keeper as well.

Sachin signalled for Emily to run, they made two before the ball was hunted down and returned.

Lisa Brunt tried her tactic one more time as she bowled her last ball. Sachin had predicted that she would do so. He moved his back foot like lightning backwards and across towards off stump. In one movement he was able to place his bat underneath the flying snowy ball and lift it back over and behind him the wicket keeper, umpire and the boundary. Leaving Lisa Brunt simply applauding the shot and shaking her head. Six!

As the bowlers changed and the fielders switched positions, Energetic Emily greeted Sachin in the middle with excitement.

They both glanced at the scoreboard:

Score: Skaggyness 147 for 7 off 90 balls. Beston lead by 27 runs with 10 balls remaining.

"Ok," Sachin opened this conversation with Emily, which was accompanied with panting and two racing heart beats. "We can do this! I need to keep hitting fours and run for everything we can,"

"But I am on strike now," Emily reminded him as if he would forget.

"I know."

"What should I do?"

"Just play the ball as you see it. If you have to leave it, leave it. If you can hit it, hit it. I will be ready," Sachin insisted.

The last ten balls had been saved for Chris Stokes to bowl. Chris Stokes was Beston's most famous player. Chris

Stokes had won the Beston Player of the year award. Not only a dangerous player but he had been known to win matches on his own. "It's all over little man," he whispered to Sachin as he caught the ball and walked to the spot that he would start his run-up.

Emily was on strike. 'Ten balls' thought Sachin. 'Just ten balls left,'

# Chapter 18

Mithali Goswami was anticipating the next tenfold deliveries. "So, Beston have left the last ten balls for Chris Stokes, nicknamed Venom! So nothing for Emily Burton to worry about. Here he comes."

Emily was expecting a really hard and fast ball; she wasn't left disappointed. She awkwardly appeared to throw her bat at the ball defending herself from this acid globe. The ball flew away towards the boundary and her heart soared as she watched it fly.

Goswami noted her actions, "She's somehow got hold of that on the swing…Oh no way. No, no way, that is remarkable! You cannot do that Heather Taylor that is a superhuman catch. Look at the crowd reaction to that catch, they are on their feet. That is one of the greatest catches of all time at any level! Next to me I think Phil is speechless."

"I am trying to take in what I have just seen. Heather Taylor was standing a little out of position as Emily Burton swung Chris Stokes into the leg side, Taylor back pedalled rapidly, arched herself backwards, stretched out her right hand and plucked the ball from the air in front of a disbelieving crowd. Even Taylor shook her head and looked as though she could scarcely work out how she had done it – and this match has a cherished moment," Agnew reflected.

Emily hung her head. She walked off. She left her helmet on, desperate not to make eye contact with anyone. Sachin trotted over to her. He told her she was very unlucky.

"I've let you down Sachin," she claimed.

"No, it's just cricket! You did brilliantly," he insisted.

She paused her stroll for a second and gave him a quick hug. She wished him luck before she broke into a sprint to the pavilion.

With just nine balls left and a new batsman on strike, the crowd had decided any vain hope of a Skaggyness victory had gone.

Score: Skaggyness 147 for 8 off 91 balls. Beston lead by 27 runs with 9 balls remaining.

Billy Ranger was next in. He was a bull as he entered the ring searching frantically for the matador.

He was swinging his bat all the way out to the crease. In fact he was swinging his bat so much by the time he reached Sachin he commented to him.

"My arms are aching already." He continued, "They all say we can't win Sachin. But I think you are more likely to know."

"We can still win but we need to score runs and fast."

Billy asked the question Sachin hoped to hear. "What do you need me to do to help?"

"Just try and get me back on strike with a little tap and a quick run."

"Ok will do," Billy was full of promise. "Can I use the FORCE?" he asked sniggering.

"If you can. It would be a good time!" Sachin assured him.

"I have got a bad feeling about this!" Billy whispered to himself.

Sachin was mindful that Billy had never played in a cricket match before.

Billy was playing Sachin's words over and over in his mind. 'A little tap and a quick run, a little tap and a quick run'.

Stokes was soon steaming in, now he was the bull.

As the bull came towards Billy he angled his bat with the handle well forward over the ball as it made contact. The ball dropped to the floor and Billy ran. Sachin ran. Sharma, who was the closest fielder ran. Sharma picked up the ball and turned to throw it at the stumps.

Surely this was a run out.

As the two batsmen crossed they had made a run. The ball hit the stumps without Billy making his ground. He was out!

Score: Skaggyness 148 for 9 off 92 balls. Beston lead by 26 runs with 8 balls remaining.

Stokes faced up to Sachin and breathed, "You've lost little man!"

Sachin didn't react as he watched Billy trudge off a little confused.

Agnew noted, "Well this match is going the way we expected now. Beston showing their dominance over a poor Skaggyness team. It's been a cute try from young Sachin Dulkar but class will tell."

Where Billy was a bull, the incoming George was a bright eyed rabbit. George hopped into the arena somewhat cautiously. He seemed to criss-cross his walk; stalling for time?

Sachin could see just how nervous this young kit was. Sachin just asked George if he could hit the ball as hard as he could if he was on strike and run when he told him to run. George agreed with a petrified submissive yelp.

Meanwhile, a disappointed but proud Mr and Mrs Dulkar sat rather calmer than previously. They knew their son had done everything he could to win this match. The crowd appreciated how good his effort had been. The crowd were drifting off for drinks as they all seemed to have accepted what seemed inevitable; a Beston victory.

Sachin was still in-the-zone.

Stokes began his run-up, as Skaggyness were now clinging on by the flimsiest skin of their teeth.

Stokes had believed it was just a matter of time now and bowled a fairly gentle ball giving Sachin a chance to fall into a huge backswing motion which saw his hands over the flight of the ball. In a swooping smooth hit his front foot zipped back and towards his left-side, this made his chest ball height. The snap of his bat connecting with the ball saw it fly, sprout wings and soar way over the boundary for six!

Stokes grimaced at Sachin. His magnificent stroke seemed to make Stokes angry. Sachin ignored him, he was busy checking the maths.

Score: Skaggyness 154 for 9 off 93 balls. Beston lead by 20 runs with 7 balls remaining.

Stokes picked up the pace with his next ball. Sachin timed his front foot drive to perfection. Stokes had given him a fast full-length ball and Sachin showed his masterful nature to the ball by simply pushing to the boundary for four.

Score: Skaggyness 158 for 9 off 94 balls. Beston lead by 16 runs with 6 balls remaining.

Stokes sent down a shorter ball that found Sachin defending, but he managed to push it a few metres. Would that be far enough?

# CHAPTER 19

"Run! George run!" Sachin cried.

As Kaf Rabada this time ran to pick the ball up, it should have been a full gone conclusion for the fall of the final wicket as a run out. George had been too slow to begin his run and he had barely started his sprint before Sachin, ever alert, had already made his ground.

George looked quite a sight: with pads that were too big for him, a helmet that made his brain rattle inside it, a bat that made him look tiny and a shirt that was clearly more suited to his dad's frame than his. Rabada caught sight off this tortoise paced waddler. He paused for a giggle at the work of moving art pegging across him. His giggle made him drop the ball. It took him a split second to recover. He then majestically threw the ball towards the stumps.

George however had seen him drop the ball and ran faster with a heart that was also clearly three or four sizes too big for him. He catapulted himself forward, just as Rabada released his grip. In flight the two, ball and player, raced for the landing strip. He hit the middle stump with a swirling uppercut sending it sprawling.

Mthuru-Bailey insisted to the raging Beston team that George had made his ground. His bat had touched down a nanosecond before the ball punched the stump clean. NOT OUT!

Score: Skaggyness 159 for 9 off 95 balls. Beston lead by 15 runs with 5 balls remaining.

The commentators were being forced to rethink an alternative ending to this match.

"Well I never. I was sure he was out!"

"Me too! I was convinced! Beston had surely wrapped this match up with the expected result," Mithali Goswami echoed the thoughts of her co-commentator.

"With young Dulkar on strike, the rate he has been scoring, this match is not quite over," suggested Phil Agnew.

Stokes walked to the other end of the shaven strip of grass ready to complete the last five of the balls of the match. Once again he took the opportunity to place Sachin in a shadow and to state clearly and calmly, "You're gone little man."

Stokes walked away from him. Sachin thanked him as he moved.

Stokes turned and began his run-up. Sachin was waiting. As the Sun continued to bake, the master chef of the crease was busy cooking up a winning recipe. Could he do it? Can he do it? Will he do it? One or two members of the crowd were beginning to ask the question. They had waited all afternoon for the inevitable result. Such was the skill and judgement of Sachin Dulkar, the unthinkable was just possible.

Stokes steamed in. He launched his rocket straight at Sachin who stepped forward and gave an almighty swing with his cricket hammer. Sachin had been Thor like all day. The Sun had been sapping everyone's energy. Sachin just seemed to be getting stronger with every ball he faced. He sent this ball heading for yet another boundary, high in the air.

Mithali Goswami shared her view of it, "Now then is this it, is this it, he's under it, he's got it! Sharma has caught it! Oh he has fallen and now Roy Jason has it in his hands. He's out right? Dulkar is out caught Sharma or caught Jason? Phil the umpire is not signalling out so what's occurring? Phil, please explain."

"Ok. I am just watching a replay here that only I can see. Okay the umpire has clearly seen what I have just watched a second time. As Sharma took the catch he stepped back onto the boundary and then flipped the ball to Roy Jason who also caught it."

"So that's out!?" insisted Goswami, "We can all go home now, Beston have won."

"Not quite Mithali. Because Sharma has stepped back onto the boundary rope he has accidentally taken the ball over the boundary and therefore out of the field of play. It's a six and wonderboy is not out!"

"Would you believe it!"

Score: Skaggyness 165 for 9 off 96 balls. Beston lead by 9 runs with 4 balls remaining.

Stokes then delivered Sachin an impossible ball. He played at it but the bat turned in his hand. He played and missed. Straight into the gloves of Josh Bairstow who tried to claim he was out! The whole Beston team was desperate to get Sachin out. They screamed their appeal so loud they probably heard it in Australia!

Umpire Heyhoe-Flint stood motionless.

Skaggyness 165 for 9 off 97 balls. Beston lead by 9 runs with 3 balls remaining.

Stokes ran in once more confident that Sachin was a spent force now and couldn't make the runs he needed. Sachin needed boundaries. He'd already seen George run…erm well make a quick waddle.

Stokes bowled a short ball. Sachin moved forward and met the ball with the full face of his bat. It sped towards the boundary but a salmon like leap from Holder prevented it from just reaching the four mark. As George and Sachin ran, Sachin shouted to George for a second run. Holder threw the ball back to where Sachin was running. Sachin made it. George was only half way back down the pitch but he made it before the Beston players could react.

Score: Skaggyness 168 for 9 off 98 balls. Beston lead by 6 runs with 2 balls remaining.

"Well we are now down to this. This is possible!" declared Agnew.

"I can't quite believe this match. It has been quite a surprise!" added Goswami.

"So, Skaggyness from nothing have got within touching distance of their first victory over Beston, at any level, since 1971. This is the mighty, mighty Beston well and truly beaten by Sachin Dulkar IF he can score 7 off the last two balls."

Agnew, "Can he do it?"

Goswami, "I don't think he can, especially with this running mate, but it has been a great match, just not the exhibition we were expecting." The crowd's conversations were echoing that of the commentators.

In came Stokes. Sachin counted the thunder as it stepped towards him. In came the ball. Sachin had to make a quick decision. The ball was heading straight for his wicket. It took all his power to just block the ball from striking the target. He shouted to George not to run. The ball was quickly fielded and the Beston players started to congratulate each other. They were shaking hands and patting each other on the back. Sachin stretched his arms in disgust. The crowd thought it was over.

The umpires reminded the Beston players that there was one ball left.

Score: Skaggyness 168 for 9 off 99 balls. Beston lead by 6 runs with 1 ball remaining.


George and Sachin had a quick chat. George asked if they had lost. Sachin insisted they hadn't. Sachin explained he had to get seven off the last ball. George insisted that even he knew that was impossible. Sachin insisted that this match was not over. "If I can't win, I want to draw. Anyway they might bowl a no ball or a wide. Anything can happen in cricket. That's why it's a brilliant game!"

Sachin left George with the instruction to just run as fast as he could the moment he hit the ball.

George understood.

Sachin waited for the Beston players to reorganise themselves for the final ball. Stokes came in to bowl his last ball. Relaxed, he picked a spot for the ball to land where Sachin had shown that he couldn't get his power behind it. Sachin pounced on the bobbling ball. He did manage to hit the ball far enough to steal at least one run. George had run so fast he was now ahead of Sachin. The ball didn't come in to the stumps so Sachin bellowed for George to run for a second.

As Beston had eased off, they saw no urgency. Sachin cried for a third run. They crossed for a third time, securing three runs. George made his ground but Sachin was exhausted. He was desperately struggling with cramp. He had slowed down hugely. He took off like a slow motion Superman towards the crease as the ball flew in to the very same spot.

Even the Sun burst into a smile, not always seen over Skaggyness, as the ball struck Sachin's bat as he placed it onto the ground. The whole crowd looked gobsmacked as the ball flew across the other side of the pitch and made it to the boundary for a further four runs! The crowd went berserk. Seven off one ball! Sachin said it could be done and it was done! The scoreboard told the world the story.

Score: Skaggyness 175 for 9 off 100 balls. Beston 174 for 3 off 100 balls.

Skaggyness win by 1 run.

The crowd were in raptures. The younger elements of the crowd were running onto the field to congratulate Sachin. They were trying to lift him off his feet and carry their new hero off the field. George was getting knocked over and trampled on. Rightly so, Sachin was being lavishly applauded by everybody that could reach out to him.

Uncle Ganguly's face told the story. It was ashen.

Mr. Dulkar went over to him. He clasped his two hands onto the cheeks of a shocked Ganguly.

Mr. Dulkar gasped, "Never has your flabber been so gasted!" then he quickly made for Sachin.

As Sachin eventually reached the boundary his father was ready to greet him. The two embraced and Mr Dulkar had tears in his eyes as he bent down to his son. Sachin whispered, "That was for you dad. I love cricket and I love you!"

In one swift movement, Phil Agnew appeared from nowhere and flashed passed all the Beston players, who had quickly gone from heroes to zeros. He pushed a microphone firmly under Sachin's chin and asked him, "Well young Sachin how does it feel to beat the brilliant Beston?"

"Ok," shrugged Sachin, somewhat modestly.

"Your batting was masterful today. Where were you coached?" Agnew continued.

"He's the little master!" quipped Mr Dulkar still lurking behind his boy.

Sachin searched all around him, looking for an escape route now the cricket was over.

Phil Agnew insisted on one more question, "Is it going to be India or England for you Sachin?"

"IN-DI-A!" cried his dad.

"England. But either would be an honour!" grinned Sachin, much to his father's delight.

# CHAPTER 20

*Skaggyness Innings*

| | | | |
|---|---|---|---|
| C.Hangar | | b Rabada | 0 |
| S.Dulkar | not out | | 96 |
| K.Peters | c Bairstow | b Brunt | 20 |
| M.Murphy | run out | | 39 |
| K.Taylor | c Hafeez | b Brunt | 0 |
| M.Perry | c Bairstow | b Raj | 0 |
| S.Gilchrist | | b Raj | 4 |
| S.Archer | | b Raj | 4 |
| E.Burton | c Taylor | b Stokes | 0 |
| B.Ranger | run out | | 0 |
| G.Forest | not out | | 0 |
| *Extras* | | | *12* |

| | |
|---|---|
| Total | 175 for 9 |

| | |
|---|---|
| **Beston** | *174 – 3 (100 balls)* |
| **Skaggyness** | *175 – 9 (100 balls)* |
| **Result** | *Skaggyness won by 1 run.* |

# Glossary

**Ball:** White for one-day matches and red for first-class matches. It weighs 5.5 ounces (5 ounces for women's cricket and 4.75 ounces for junior cricket).

**Batter:** Another word for a person who is batting, first used in 1773. Also something you fry fish in.

**Beamer:** A ball that does not bounce (usually accidently) and passes the batsman at or about head height. If aimed straight at the batsman by a fast bowler, this is a very dangerous delivery (thought of as unsporting).

**Bouncer:** A short-pitched ball which passes the batsman at head or chest height.

**Boundary:** The perimeter of a cricket field, or the act of the batsman scoring a six or a four (e.g. "Sachin hammered three boundaries").

**Cow corner:** An unconventional fielding position, more commonly found in the lower reaches of the game, on the midwicket/long-on boundary. The term is thought to have originated at Dulwich College where there was the corner of a field containing cows on that side of the playing area. Fielders were dispatched to the "cow corner".

**Extras:** Runs not scored by batsmen. There are four common extras – byes, leg byes, wides and no-balls. In some places, like Australia, they are known as sundries.

**Leg-Before Wicket (LBW):** Leg before wicket (lbw) is one of the ways in which a batsman can be dismissed. A complex rule but simply put, you cannot be out if the ball pitched *outside* the line of leg stump; you cannot be out if the ball hits you outside the line of off stump unless you are offering no stroke.

Aside from that, if it hits you in line, the only decision the umpire makes is to say whether the ball is going on to hit the stumps or not.

**Leg-bye**: When the ball deflects off the pad and the batsmen run. A shot must be offered to the ball. Leg-byes do not count against the bowler.

**No-ball:** An illegitimate delivery, usually when the bowler has overstepped on the front crease.

**Off-side:** The side of the pitch which is to batsman's right (if right-handed), or left (if left-handed).

**On-side:** The same as the leg-side.

**Out:** There are ten possible ways of being out: bowled, caught, hit wicket, lbw, stumped, timed out, handled the ball, obstruction, hit the ball twice, and run out.

To be out "retired out" is gaining in currency and popularity and counts as a dismissal, unlike "retired hurt".

**Rope:** Used to mark the perimeter of the field. If the ball crosses or hits the rope, a boundary will be signalled.

**Run-chase:** Generally the fourth innings of a first-class or Test match, and the latter stages of a one-day game, when the match situation has been reduced to a set figure for victory, in a set time or maximum number of overs.

**Square leg:** A fielder who stands on the leg side of the wicket and quite close to the striking batsman.

**Strike rate:** The number of runs a batsman scores per hundred balls; the number of deliveries a bowler needs to take his wickets.

**Throwing:** To deliver a ball from a bowler, an illegal bowling action in which the arm is straightened during the delivery.

**Wicket:** One of those key words that is central to the game of cricket. The word can be used to describe the 22 yards between the stumps, the stumps collectively (bails included), the act of hitting these stumps and so dismissing the batsman, and oddly, the act of not being out. Plus any other use you care to think of.

**Wide:** A delivery that passes illegally wide of the wicket, scoring an extra for the batting side. A wide does not count as one of the six valid deliveries that must be made in each over – an extra ball must be bowled for each wide. The umpire will single this by stretching his arms out horizontally, an extra will be added to the total and the ball will be bowled again.

**Yorker:** A full pitched (usually fast) delivery that is aimed at the batsman's toes and/or the base of the stumps. If the ball is swinging, these can be the most lethal delivery in the game or provide a good batsman with a boundary if the ball is not delivered correctly.

 Matador

For exclusive discounts on Matador titles,
sign up to our occasional newsletter at
troubador.co.uk/bookshop